Another Sommer-Time Story

No Longer A Dilly Dally

By Carl Sommer
Illustrated by Kennon James

Advance
PUBLISHING, INC • HOUSTON

Permissions
Advance Publishing, Inc.
6950 Fulton St.
Houston, TX 77022

http://www.advancepublishing.com

First Edition
Printed in Singapore

Library of Congress Cataloging-in-Publication Data

Sommer, Carl, 1930-
    No longer a Dilly Dally / by Carl Sommer ; illustrated by Kennon James. – 1st ed.
        p.   cm. – (Another Sommer-time story)
    Summary: The Dilly Dally family likes to play first, but after barely surviving a hard winter they realize that the Work Play family's way makes more sense.
    ISBN 1-57537-001-8 (hc : alk. paper). – ISBN 1-57537-053-0 (lib. bdg. : alk. paper)
    [1. Insects–Fiction. 2. Work–Fiction. 3. Conduct of life–Fiction.] I. James, Kennon, ill. II. Title. III. Series: Sommer, Carl, 1930- Another Sommer-time story.
    PZ7.S696235No 1997
    [E]–dc20   96-24351
                                                                        CIP
                                                                        AC

Another Sommer-Time Story

No Longer A Dilly Dally

Once there was a great city of ants—big and busy.

One day, two families decided to leave the crowded city and move to the country. They were Family Work Play and Family Dilly Dally.

Family Dilly Dally packed all their things. They were eager to find a new place where they would have lots of fun.

Family Work Play also packed all their things. They were sad to be leaving their friends in the city, but happy to be starting a new home in the country.

Both families waved good-bye to their friends, and off they went—out into the big, wide world.

Papa Work Play immediately gathered his family together. "It takes a lot of hard work to build a new home. Let's get started right away."

Papa Dilly Dally immediately found a place to rest. "We have plenty of time to build a new home. Let's rest first and have some fun."

Family Work Play decided to look for a place where they could find lots of food. They searched long and hard until they found just the right place to build their home.

"This is an excellent place for us to find food," said Mama Work Play. Papa immediately began making plans for their new home.

After a time of rest and play, Family Dilly Dally decided to look for a place where they could have plenty of fun. They searched for just the right place to build their house.

They were excited when they found a large shade tree next to a beautiful lake. Although they had to walk far to get food, it was a perfect place for them to have lots of fun.

Meanwhile Family Work Play went right to work. In their home it was early to bed and early to rise.

"We are Family Work Play!" Papa would say. "And that means we work first, then play. Every day we will have time to relax and play, but we must always do our work first."

In the mornings they dug their basement, and in the afternoons they gathered food.

"In a few months it will get bitter cold," Papa warned. "Let's work hard now so when winter comes we'll have a nice home and plenty of food."

In the evenings they relaxed and played.

All through the hot summer months, Family
Work Play worked long and hard.

By late summer their house was almost finished, and their basement was nearly full. Still every day they gathered more food to make sure they would have enough for the coming winter.

Things were much different by the lake. Since Family Dilly Dally did not like hard work, they quickly built a tiny house. They wanted a nice, big home...but they would build it later. For now they just wanted to have fun—and lots of it.

In the evenings they stayed up late watching their favorite TV shows.

Since they went to bed late, they slept late. Often they did not even bother going to bed.

When they finally did wake up, it was already hot outside...much too hot to work. So they began their day by relaxing and playing under the big shade tree.

They waited until the cool evenings to look for something to eat. And since food was so far away, it was not long before someone would say, "It's getting dark. Let's go home."

"That's a good idea!" they all would agree.

And so it went—day after day, week after week. Family Dilly Dally gathered only enough food for the next day.

By the end of summer, Family Dilly Dally's small house was still unfinished. And they had no food stored for the winter.

But they had lots of fun.

Every day, as Family Work Play went to gather food, Family Dilly Dally would call out to them, "Come! Play ball with us."

"We can't play now," the hard-working ants would say. "We must work first, then we can play."

"Don't be so foolish!" Family Dilly Dally would say. "Be like us! We play first, then we work."

"Oh no! In our family, we work first."

Mama Work Play felt sad for Family Dilly Dally. "We must warn our friends that unless they work first, things will be very hard for them when the cold winter comes."

Mama Work Play went to Family Dilly Dally's home and knocked on the door.

"Come in," called Mama Dilly Dally from her couch. "What brings you here?"

"I've noticed that you're not preparing for the coming winter," Mama Work Play warned. "It's going to get very cold, and then it will be hard to find food."

"Oh, don't worry about us," said Mama Dilly Dally sweetly. "Our family just loves to play. There's still plenty of time to get food for the winter. Anyway, thanks for coming."

Mama Work Play left the house very sad. She felt sorry for Family Dilly Dally because she knew they were going to suffer much during the coming cold winter.

When fall arrived, Family Work Play's basement was completely filled with food.

"I'm proud of the way you've worked," Mama Work Play told her children. "Now we have plenty of food for the winter."

"And we've finished building our home," said Papa Work Play. "Let's have some fun."

"Hooray!" shouted the children.

They packed some games and a basket full of food. Then they headed for the lake.

They had a wonderful time at the lake.

"Since we're well prepared for winter," said Papa Work Play, "we'll have much more time to relax and play."

Now Family Work Play had fun.

One windy day Papa Dilly Dally called his family together and sadly announced, "Fall is here, and that means we must begin to get food for the winter."

"Oh noooo...!" they all complained. "It's getting cold outside, and the food is far away!"

"We played first," Papa told them. "Now we must work!"

They finally headed out to search for food, but they moaned and groaned the whole time.

Now Family Dilly Dally had lots of work.

Wintertime found Family Work Play in their warm, cozy home. No longer did they have to go out into the cold to find something to eat—their basement was full of food.

Now Family Work Play had lots of fun.

Wintertime found Family Dilly Dally in the cold outdoors. Leaves covered the ground, and it became very hard to find food.

Still every day they had to go out and search for something to eat. Now they had no time to play.

Soon it became bitter cold, and Family Dilly Dally had to dig through ice and snow to find food.

Every day it was the same—searching and digging, digging and searching—and still their tummies were never quite full. Although they grumbled and complained, it did them no good.

Now it was *all* work...and *no* play.

"I've got a great idea!" said Papa Dilly Dally.
"I'll ask Family Work Play for help. They have
plenty of food."

When he went into their house, he was
surprised by how nice and warm it was. "My,
what a beautiful home you have!"

"Thank you," they said.

"Could you please give us food for the winter?"
Papa Dilly Dally asked. "It's much too cold
outside to be searching for food."

"I'm sorry," said Papa Work Play, "but we don't have enough food for both our families."

Papa Dilly Dally left the house very sad.

"I feel sorry for them," said Mama Work Play. "It's hard to find food in the cold winter. Shouldn't we *try* to feed them?"

"I feel sorry for them too," said Papa. "But if we feed them, they might never learn to work first. Besides, if they work very hard, they will find enough food—even if it gets icy cold."

In the middle of winter it turned icy cold. The snow was deep and finding food was harder than ever. Still every day—from sunrise to sunset— Family Dilly Dally had to trudge a long way through the deep snow to search for food.

Day after day, week after week, Family Dilly Dally shivered as they dug in the snow. They were always hungry and cold...and thankful to find even a crumb.

All the fun things that they had done were long forgotten. Now it was nothing but work... work...and more work!

Little by little the snow melted, and the frosty fields turned green again. Spring had arrived, and not a moment too soon for Family Dilly Dally.

It was not easy living through the cold, harsh winter. But they learned a lesson—the hard way.

Papa Dilly Dally gathered his family together. He cleared his throat and slowly said, "I have something very important to say. I am no longer...a Dilly Dally!"

The kids were shocked. "What do you mean, Papa?"

Papa put on a new hat—a work hat—and then explained.

"I'm going to have a new name! We were foolish for playing first, instead of working first."

Mama agreed. "I don't want to be a Dilly Dally either!"

"Neither do we!" shouted the kids.

Just then some old friends came by.

"Hi there!" It was Family Work Play. "How's everything going, Mr. Dilly Dally?"

Papa pointed to his new work hat and said, "I'm no longer a Dilly Dally!"

"Neither are we!" shouted Mama and the kids. "We're changing our name."

Papa stood real tall. "From now on our new name will be . . . Family Work First!"

"Hooray!" cheered Mama and the kids.

Family Work First wasted no time, but immediately went to work. They began building a new home right next to Family Work Play.

In the mornings they dug their basement and built their home. In the afternoons they gathered food...

. . . and in the evenings they relaxed and played.
Best of all, from that day on they lived up to
their new name—Family WORK FIRST!